D0581702

This Ladybird Book belongs to:

_____

_____

_____

_____

Retold by Ronne P. Randall
Illustrated by Stephen Holmes

Cover illustration by John Gurney

Copyright © Ladybird Books USA 1997

Originally published in the United Kingdom by Ladybird Books Ltd © 1993

First American edition by Ladybird Books,
a division of Penguin Books USA Inc.
375 Hudson Street, New York, New York 10014

Printed in Great Britain
1 3 5 7 9 10 8 6 4 2

ISBN 0–7214–5710–X

FAVORITE TALES

The Little Red Hen

nce upon a time, there was
a little red hen who lived on
a farm.

One morning, the little red hen
decided to plant some grains of wheat.
She took the wheat to the other
animals in the farmyard.

"Who will help me plant these grains of wheat?" the little red hen asked her friends.

"Not I," said the cat.

"Not I," said the rat.

"Not I," said the pig.

"Then I shall plant the wheat myself," said the little red hen.

And that's just what she did. She planted the grains in a neat row in the sunniest part of the field.

The little red hen looked after the wheat very carefully. She watered it every day and watched it grow.

At last the wheat was tall, strong, and golden. The little red hen knew it was ready to be cut.

"Who will help me cut this wheat?"
the little red hen asked the other
animals in the farmyard.

"Not I," said the cat.

"Not I," said the rat.

"Not I," said the pig.

"Then I shall cut the wheat myself," said the little red hen.

And that's just what she did. She went out into the field and carefully cut down each stalk of golden wheat.

Then she took the wheat back to the farmyard.

"Who will help me take this wheat to the miller to be ground into flour?" the little red hen asked her friends.

"Not I," said the cat.

"Not I," said the rat.

"Not I," said the pig.

"Then I shall take the wheat to the miller myself," said the little red hen.

And that's just what she did. She carried the wheat to the mill where the miller ground it into flour. He put the flour into a sack, and the little red hen carried it back to the farmyard.

"Who will help me carry this sack of
flour to the baker to bake into bread?"
the little red hen asked the other
animals in the farmyard.

"Not I," said the cat.

"Not I," said the rat.

"Not I," said the pig.

"Then I shall take it to the baker myself," said the little red hen.

And that's just what she did. The baker made the flour into a loaf of fresh, tasty bread. The little red hen took the bread back to the farmyard.

"Who will help me eat this loaf of bread?" asked the little red hen.

"I will!" said the cat.

"I will!" said the rat.

"I will!" said the pig.

"No, you will not!" answered the little red hen. "I shall eat this fresh, tasty bread all by myself!"

And that's just what she did!

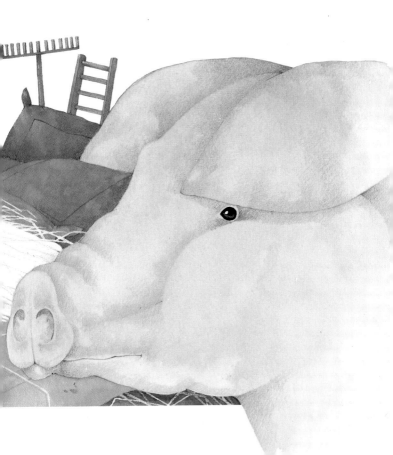

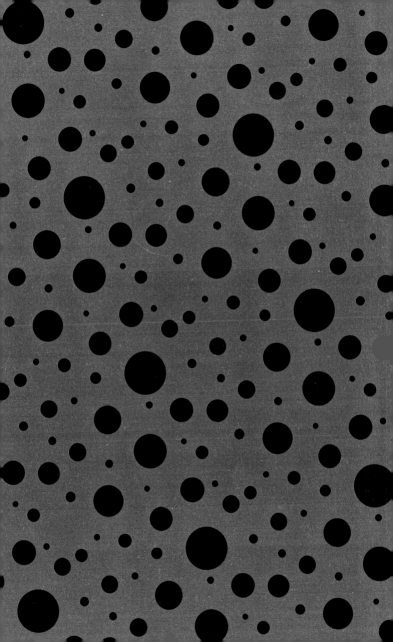